KUSA
WANTS TO PLAY!

Written by
Kathy Iorio Snow

Illustrated by
Chris Schroeder

Foreword

Enjoy another great story from Kathy Iorio's Kusa and Friends book series! KUSA WANTS TO PLAY! is a must-read to help children become more active.

As a Health and Physical Education teacher for over twenty years, I can attest to the great need for messages that encourage children to move every day.

KUSA WANTS TO PLAY! teaches two important lessons. First, it teaches readers to make the time for daily active play. This in turn can help lead one to an active lifestyle.

Secondly, this story teaches its readers the power of genuine friendships which are cultivated by actively playing together. Both are lovely life lessons!

Kathy's story makes the critical point that we all move differently as well. And the book's bonus materials are a super plus!

It is essential to help our children become physically active as they are young, which will help them on a journey of living an active lifestyle. Showing them that friends can join in this journey, as Kusa's do, makes it even more fun!

Join Kusa and Friends on this wonderful adventure!

Pamela A. Wiley, M.ED, NBCT
Health and Physical Education Teacher
Erie Public Schools, Erie, Pennsylvania

Acknowledgments

A big heartfelt thank you to my husband and best friend, Tony Snow, M.D., for his continued love and support throughout the years and to my friends, brothers, and sister for being a significant part of my journey.

My deepest gratitude to my mother for her unconditional love.

A special thanks to Amy Luce, teacher, writer, and a good friend, for her extraordinary editing support. I want to thank Chris Schroeder for his friendship and creative support for helping to make this book come to life.

Thank you to Marsha Blessing and the team at Orison Publishers, Inc. for coaching and assisting me in this publishing adventure. Their insightful input and excellent publishing expertise were invaluable and deeply appreciated.

I am most grateful to God because, with God, all things are possible; without God, none of this would be possible.

Dedication

To encourage children of all shapes, sizes, and abilities to engage in active play in some way, their way, every day.

Testimonials

Kusa Wants to Play! is an awesome story. Through play, children are active. We know that being active helps us lead healthier and happier lives. Best of all, Kusa reminds the children how easy it is to "move and groove." After the story, author Kathy Iorio shares some of the many ways children can move and play—great idea!

This book is an excellent reminder that even though we are all different, we can all play in our own way.

As Kathy says, "PLAY SOME WAY, YOUR WAY, EVERY DAY."
Great lesson, Kathy and Kusa!

Diane Lopez,
K-12 Health and Physical Education Teacher

Kathy Iorio has done it again!

What a timeless wellness-fitness lesson embedded in a fun and encouraging story. Parents will appreciate the "let's play and move" theme as a great stimulus with today's electronic and sedentary culture.

My grandchildren love Kusa's relatable and friendly personality and the bonus materials at the end of each book. Way to go, Kathy!

Bob Deppen,
PhD, MPA

Kusa was ready for
adventure and set out to
play at the watering hole.

She arrived to find
Buddy, the chirping bird,
perched on a branch;
Keekee, the giraffe,
grazing on the grass;
and Joffy, the monkey,
sitting in a tree.

"Hey, everyone! Let's play together!" Kusa said as she knelt to roll in the mud.

"Nah," Buddy said,
yawning. "I don't
want to do anything
today. I feel lazy.

Oh, shucks, Kusa thought, disappointed. She turned to Keekee. "Come on, Keekee! Let's play!"

"No," replied Keekee. "I'm tired. I just want to graze on the grass."

Oh, shucks, Kusa thought
again. "Hey, Joffy, do you
want to play?"

Sorry," said Joffy. "I just want
to sit in this tree."

Just then, Chacha
Cheetah arrived at
the watering hole.
"Hi, everyone!"
Chacha said.

Noticing Kusa's sad face, she asked, "What's wrong, Kusa?"

"I'm disappointed that no one is in the mood to play today," Kusa said.

"Hmmm," Chacha Cheetah said. "Maybe they need you to show them what you showed me about how good it feels to move and groove."

Kusa thought for a
moment, and then with a
big smile, she said, "Oh, I
remember, Chacha!"

Kusa raised her voice and said, "Hey, everyone, Chacha can run very fast! What can YOU do?"

20

"I can stretch tall,"
Keekee said.

"I can swing on branches in trees and do the funky monkey," Joffy said.

"And I love to roll and play in the mud!" Kusa said. "So, we all do different things, but we all do the same thing: we MOVE!"

"Come on, everyone! Let's run,
fly, stretch, swing, and play!"
Chacha said. "Who's in?"

The animal friends
looked at each
other and then
said, "We're in!"

Kusa grinned. "OK! Ready, set, go!" Buddy flew around the watering hole doing his new loop-the-loops and singing his happy chirping song, "Chirp, chirp, chirp, chirp, chirp!"

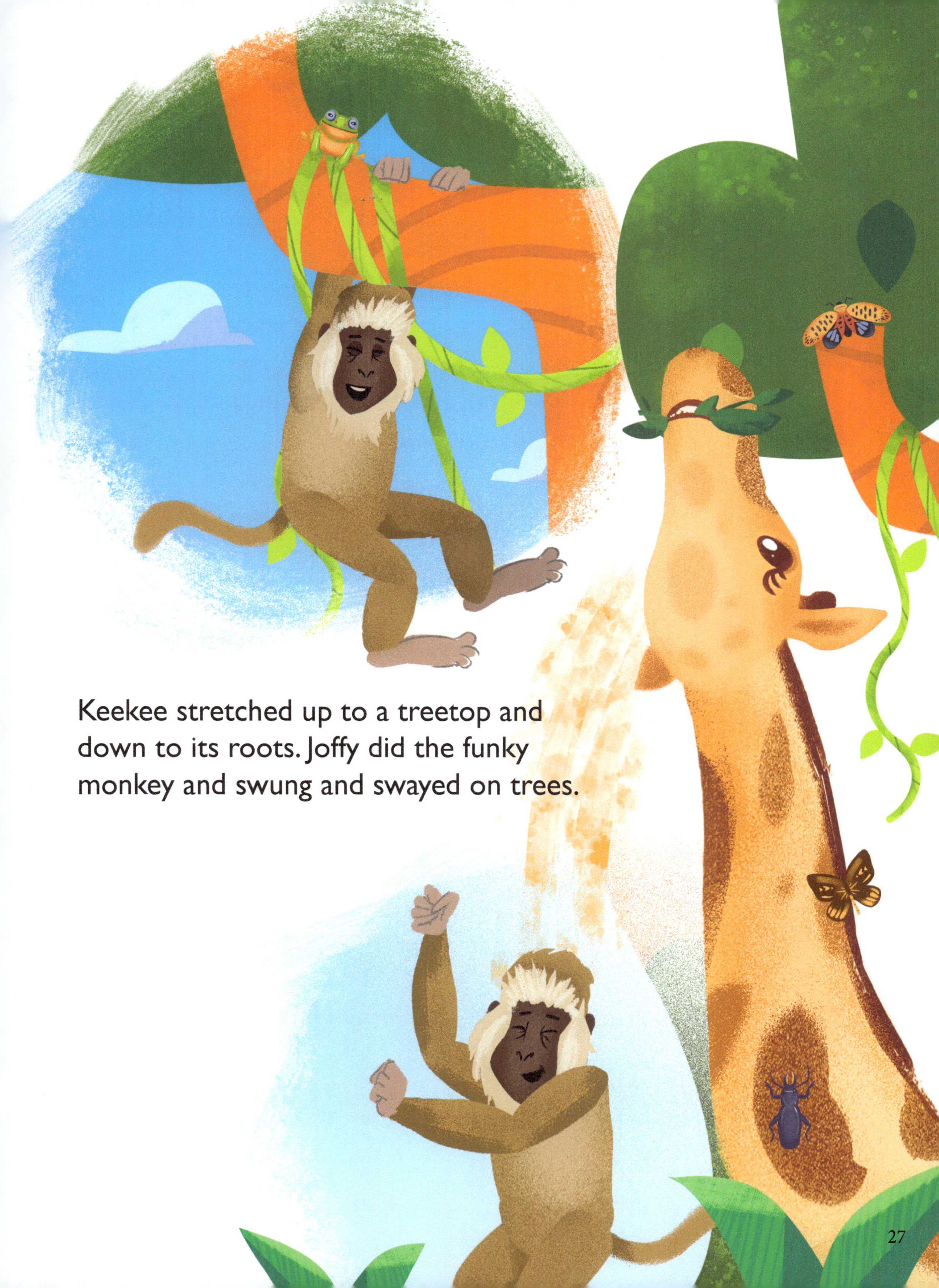

Keekee stretched up to a treetop and down to its roots. Joffy did the funky monkey and swung and swayed on trees.

Chacha ran around the watering hole as fast as lightning, and Kusa continued to roll in the mud with glee!

The animal friends had so much fun playing in their own ways, together!

After a while, they gathered around the watering hole, feeling refreshed and relaxed. "I'm not tired anymore," Buddy said.

"It always feels good to move and groove!" Keekee said excitedly. "I love doing the funky monkey and swinging on trees!" Joffy said joyfully. "And I love to run fast," Chacha said as she winked at Kusa.

"That was great!" Kusa said.
"Let's meet here tomorrow to
play again!" "Yay!" shouted the
animal friends.

As Kusa walked home, she was so glad that Chacha had reminded her of something they'd discovered: that even very different animals, like a cheetah and an elephant, can play together by movin' and groovin' in their own ways.

So, like Kusa and her animal friends, move some way, your way, every day!

LET'S TALK ACTIVE PLAY!

1. Name three ways you like to play.

2. Name three ways you like to play indoors and outdoors.

3. What are some ways you can play when you are by yourself?

4. Name three ways you can play with friends and family.

5. What are three ways you like to play when you are at school?

SOME FUN WAYS TO PLAY!

RIDE A BIKE	HIKE WITH FRIENDS AND FAMILY	SWIM	SKATE	BUILD A FORT	FLY A KITE
GO TO A PLAYGROUND	PLAY SPORTS	WALK	RUN	DANCE	GO BOWLING · SKIP
HAVE A SCAVENGER HUNT	JUMP ROPE	CREATE AN INDOOR/ OUTDOOR OBSTACLE COURSE	PLAY HOPSCOTCH		PLAY HIDE 'N' SEEK WITH FRIENDS AND FAMILY
JUMP · PLAY CATCH	HELP PLANT A GARDEN	HELP RAKE LEAVES	PLAY HULA HOOP GAMES	TOSS A FLYING DISC	
PLAY TAG	WALK THE DOG	PLAY BALL	HOP	PLAY HOT POTATO	
REACH 'N' STRETCH	BEAN-BAG TOSS	PICK BERRIES	PLAY FOLLOW THE LEADER		
PLAY DUCK, DUCK, GOOSE	PLAY RED LIGHT, GREEN LIGHT	BUILD A BLOCK TOWER	MAKE SNOW ANGELS IN THE SNOW		

CHEETAH FUN FACTS

Cheetahs are the fastest land animal on earth! They can reach speeds of 60 to 70 miles per hour. They can go from standing still to running 60 mph in three seconds!

Each cheetah has thousands of spots in a pattern! Wow, that's a lot of spots!

Cheetah males are usually more social than females. Chacha Cheetah is an exception because she enjoys her jungle friends.

Cheetahs are members of the cat family.

Cheetahs do not roar like lions; they meow, purr, and make small chirping sounds like a bird when they talk to each other.

Cheetahs do not climb.

A baby cheetah is called a cub.

Cheetahs have excellent eyesight.

BE A CRITTER CATCHER!

Find, identify, and count
the hidden critters on each page.

Longhorn Beetle

Leaf Mimic Katydid

Frog

Pleasing Fungus Beetle

Queen Alexandra's Birdwing Butterfly

Lantern Fly

Titan Beetle

Clear Winged Butterfly

Termite

Answer Key:

Pg. 6-7 Termite, LM Katydid, Longhorn Beetle, Frog, CW Butterfly Pg. 8-9 Pleasing Fungus Beetle, QAB Butterfly, Lantern Fly, Frog, LM Katydid, Termite Pg. 10-11 Titan Beetle, LM Katydid, CW Butterfly, Lantern Fly, Termite Pg. 12-13 Pleasing Fungus Beetle, Lantern Fly, QAB Butterfly, CW Butterfly, Frog, LM Katydid, Termite, Titan Beetle, Pg. 14-15 Pleasing Fungus Beetle, CW Butterfly, LM Katydid, Lantern Fly, Frog, QAB Butterfly, Termite Pg. 16-17 Frog, Titan Beetle, Lantern Fly, CW Butterfly, LM Katydid, QAB Butterfly, Pleasing Fungus Beetle, Pg. 18-19 LM Katydid, Frog, Termite, Pleasing Fungus Beetle, QAB Butterfly, Titan Beetle, Pg. 20-21 Lantern Fly, CW Butterfly, Termite, LM Katydid, Pg. 22-23 LM Katydid, Pleasing Fungus Beetle, Termite, Lantern Fly, QAB Butterfly, Frog, CW Butterfly, Pg. 24-25 Termite, Titan Beetle, CW Butterfly, Lantern Fly, QAB Butterfly, Frog, LM Katydid Pg. 26-27 Termite, LM Katydid, CW Butterfly, Frog, Lantern Fly, QAB Butterfly, Titan Beetle, Pg. 28-29 QAB Butterfly, CW Butterfly, Termite, Lantern Fly, Pleasing Fungus Beetle, Frog, LM Katydid, Pg. 30-31 Pleasing Fungus Beetle, Lantern Fly, Titan Beetle, QAB Butterfly, Termite, CW Butterfly, Frog Pg. 32-33 Frog, LM Katydid, QAB Butterfly, Termite, Lantern Fly, CW Butterfly, Longhorn Beetle

Join Kusa and Friends to learn about empowering life lessons and positive messages. Young children enjoy these life lessons and the bonus discussion questions, animal fun facts and searching for critters throughout each book.

Other Kusa And Friends books currently available.

KUSA'S Big Surprise! ISBN 978-1-7356775-1-4
KUSA Speaks Up! ISBN 978-1-7356775-3-8
KUSA Gets Her Mad Out! ISBN 978-1-7356775-4-5

Help spread the word about the Kusa and Friends series!

Have a question, idea, or comment? Contact the author at kathy@kusaandfriends.com

This series is available nationwide at fine bookstores, Amazon, and Barnes & Noble.